ANIMAL STARS
Casper in the Spotlight

PETERS

FRASER

&

DUNLOP

503/4 THE CHAMBERS
CHELSEA HARBOUR
LONDON SW10 0XF

AGENT:
ROYALTY SHEET №
PUBLICATION DATE:
CATEGORY:

Also in the Animal Stars series

ANIMAL STARS

Casper in the Spotlight

Narinder Dhami

Illustrated by Strawberrie Donnelly

Hodder
Children's
Books

a division of Hodder Headline plc

**With thanks to Gill Raddings of Stunt Dogs
for reviewing the film and animal training information
within this book.**

Copyright © 1999 Narinder Dhami
Illustrations copyright © 1999 Strawberrie Donnelly

First published in Great Britain in 1999
by Hodder Children's Books

A Catalogue record for this book is available from the British Library

ISBN 0 340 74401 4

Typeset by Avon Dataset Ltd, Bidford-on-Avon, Warks

Printed and bound in Great Britain by
The Guernsey Press Co. Ltd, Channel Isles

Hodder Children's Books
a division of Hodder Headline plc
338 Euston Road
London NW1 3BH

1

The house was on fire. Smoke was billowing from the bedroom windows, and flames were leaping and licking around the upstairs rooms, bright orange and red against the dark night sky. A crowd of people had gathered to watch what was going on, but they hurried out of the way as a fire engine raced up the road, its siren blaring.

"Hang on, son!" One of the firemen jumped down, and grabbed a young boy who was fighting his way through the crowd, towards the door of the blazing house. "What do you think you're doing? You can't go in there!"

"Let go of me!" Paul shouted, his face pale with anxiety. "My brother's inside!"

And he tore himself out of the fireman's grasp, and ran straight towards the burning house . . .

"Oh, rats!" Kim groaned, as the theme music and credits of *North Park Avenue* began to roll, a split-second before Paul got to the door. "Why do they always stop at the exciting bits!"

"Don't be a wally," her older brother Luke told her, as the commercials started. "They want to make sure you watch it again next time, don't they?"

"I *know* that." Kim stroked the shaggy-haired dog lying on her lap, and Spike blinked adoringly up at her. The Millers' other two dogs: Harry, a Jack Russell, and Casper, a Golden retriever, were asleep on the rug in front of the fire. "It's still really irritating though!"

"Well, *North Park Avenue* certainly looks like an interesting street to live in," Kim's mother said dryly. "I've only been watching the programme for the last two weeks, and so far there's been a car crash, a wedding, a kidnapping and a fire!"

"That's why it's the best soap on TV, Mum," Kim pointed out, "There's always something going on!"

"Some of the characters are a bit naff though," Luke said, pulling a face. "That kid Paul really gets on my nerves."

"Paul's brilliant!" Kim said indignantly. "Didn't you see the episode where he found his baby sister when she got lost? Everyone was talking about it!"

"This Paul leads an exciting life," their father said with a twinkle in his eyes. "If he's not finding his missing sister, he's saving his brother from a burning house!"

"Paul's big brother Matt's always getting into trouble," Kim explained, "And Paul has to keep on sorting him out." She glanced cheekily at her brother. "A bit like me and Luke, really!"

"Stop me if I laugh too hard," Luke said scathingly.

"It's a bit unusual to have a *nice* person like Paul in a soap," their father remarked, "Usually everyone's lying and cheating and doing things they shouldn't be!"

"That's why everyone likes him, Dad." Kim

suddenly sat up in her armchair, and had to clutch at Spike to stop him from sliding off her lap. "Look, Casper's ad's on again!"

"Good one!" said Kim's father, looking pleased. "That's the fourth time it's been on tonight."

Casper blinked as he heard his name mentioned, and sat up, wagging his big, feathery tail slowly from side to side, his liquid dark eyes enquiring.

"You're on TV again, Casper!" Kim told him with a grin.

Although the Millers had seen the commercial for *Woof* dog biscuits several times already, they all sat and watched it intently. On the TV screen, Casper pushed open the kitchen door, and trotted into the room, sniffing slowly at all the cupboards as he went. Then he pawed at a cupboard door, opened it, dragged out a box of Woof biscuits and carried it over to a bowl in the corner. He emptied the box into the bowl, then took it back, put it in the cupboard and shut the door. Then he wolfed down all the biscuits. The commercial ended with the owner coming home, being amazed that the box is empty, and getting a new one out of her shopping bag.

"*Woof*," said the voice-over, "So good your dog won't want to wait!"

"Well done, Casper!" Kim told the retriever. Casper climbed to his feet eagerly, and went over to her, brushing his golden coat against her legs and sniffing at Spike in a friendly way. Harry, who was definitely the bossiest and nosiest of the three dogs, also sat up to see what was going on. "You were brilliant!"

"With a little help from me, of course!" Kim's father pointed out.

Kim's parents, Chris and Rachel Miller, ran an agency called *Animal Stars* from their home, which trained animals for TV and film work. Casper and Harry were both highly trained dogs who had done lots of this kind of work, and Spike, who had come to live with the Millers only a month or two before, was also being groomed for stardom. Kim loved helping out with the agency work whenever she could, and wanted to be an animal trainer herself when she grew up.

"I still can't believe that Casper's going to be in *North Park Avenue!*" Kim said breathlessly, as she rumpled the retriever's shaggy coat, "It's going to be *so* cool!"

"He's only appearing in three or four episodes," her mother pointed out.

"I don't care," Kim retorted, "He's going to be acting with Paul – it'll be brilliant!"

"You mean Jamie Marshall, the actor who *plays* Paul," her mother corrected her.

Kim shrugged. "Yeah, whatever. I'm dying to meet him!"

"I bet you any money he's not like Paul at all," Luke remarked, "No-one could be as annoying as that goody-goody little creep!"

"He seemed nice enough when Casper and I met him recently," his mother said. The Golden retriever had already met the actors he'd be working with at rehearsals.

"Luke's just jealous because Paul – I mean, Jamie – has got loads of fans!" Kim grinned. "I can't *wait* until filming starts in two days' time!"

"Lucky it's half-term, and you're not at school," her father remarked, "Or you wouldn't have been able to go."

Kim quite often went along with one of her parents when they went to the local TV studios on a job, but sometimes they had to travel to other parts of the country for filming, and often they had to stay away overnight. Then Kim couldn't go with them, because of school. But, by a lucky chance, not only was she on holiday this time, but the location scenes for *North Park Avenue* were going to be filmed only a few miles from the Millers' house, which stood on the edge of a large city called Highbridge, surrounded by beautiful countryside. Kim was particularly excited because some of the scenes for *North Park Avenue* were going to be filmed at night, and she'd never been on a night shoot before.

"Are you coming to watch the filming, Luke?" his mother asked.

Luke yawned. "I might." Luke was almost as interested in *Animal Stars* as Kim was, but now he was nearly fourteen, he thought it was much cooler to pretend that he didn't really care that much about it. "If I haven't got anything better to do."

"If you can't find any girls to chase, you mean?" Kim asked with a wicked grin. She thought her brother's new-found interest in girls was hilarious. Luke turned bright red, and chucked a cushion at her. It missed and hit Spike instead, who jumped off Kim's lap and barked.

"Sorry, Spike," Luke apologised. "I was aiming it at motormouth over there!"

Kim pulled a cross-eyed face at him, then turned to her mother.

"Mum, I'm *dying* to tell everyone at school that *North Park Avenue* is coming to film near here. When can I say something?"

"Well, you know it's supposed to be kept pretty low-key," her mother replied with a frown. "The director doesn't want lots of people turning up to have a look. It makes filming on location difficult if there's a big audience."

Kim sighed. "Oh, all right," she muttered. "I won't say a word."

"Even to Sarah?" her mother asked with a smile.

Kim blushed. Sarah Ramsay was her best mate, and she told her *everything*. "Well, I did sort of mention it to Sarah . . . But she won't tell anyone," she added hastily.

"Big mouth!" Luke said gleefully, and Kim glared at him.

"To be honest, I don't think it matters much," their mother said. "I had a call from the local newspaper this morning – they know something's going on, and that *Animal Stars* is involved.

I didn't tell them anything, but I wouldn't be surprised if there's something about the filming in the paper tomorrow night."

"So I *can* tell everyone at school tomorrow?" Kim asked eagerly, slipping her arms round Casper's neck. The big dog leaned against her legs, and thumped his tail on the carpet.

Her mother shook her head. "No, don't. They'll find out soon enough."

"OK," Kim agreed reluctantly. She gave Casper a hug, and the dog licked her chin gently. "You're going to be brilliant, Casper!" she whispered in the dog's ear, "And you and Paul – I mean, you and Jamie – are going to be great mates! I just know it."

"Did you see *North Park Avenue* last night?" Sarah asked eagerly as she and Kim walked to school on Friday morning. "D'you think Paul will be able to save Matt from the fire?"

"Oh, sure he will," Kim assured her, "Paul can do anything! Anyway," she grinned at her friend, "Matt and Paul are going to be filming with Casper tomorrow, so they both *have* to survive the fire!"

"I can't wait to meet Paul – I mean, Jamie Marshall," Sarah sighed. "This is going to be the most exciting half-term ever!"

"Make sure you come to our house early tomorrow morning," Kim told her, "Because we've got to be on set by seven o'clock." After a good deal of persuasion from Kim, her mother had agreed to take both Kim and Sarah with her to the *North Park Avenue* filming location, but they were under strict instructions to behave themselves, and keep well out of everyone's way. Kim had been out on so many jobs with her parents, she knew exactly how to behave, but this was Sarah's first visit to a TV shoot.

"Oh, I'm so excited, I'll probably be awake all night!" Sarah told her with a grin. She was the complete opposite of Kim; short and dark-haired, while Kim was tall and blonde. Sarah was also very easygoing, while Kim had inherited her mother's famous temper. Kim didn't lose her cool very often, but when she did, even Sarah found it difficult to calm her down. "I think I'll faint with excitement when I see Jamie Marshall for the first time!"

"Oh, yeah, that'll impress him!" Kim

snorted, and the two girls giggled.

"It must be weird for Jamie, acting in a soap," Sarah remarked thoughtfully, "I mean, he's only twelve, a few years older than us."

"He doesn't have to go to school either!" Kim said with a groan, as they walked up to the gates of Hightown Primary. "He has a private tutor on the set."

"Lucky him!" Sarah said enviously. "I wonder if he'll like Casper?"

"Oh, he will!" Kim said confidently, "Everyone does." Casper was popular wherever he went, because, despite his size, he had a very gentle, loveable personality. Kim was certain that he and Jamie Marshall would get on brilliantly right from the start.

"How's the problem page going, by the way?" Sarah asked, as they went into the playground. Kim had an 'animals problem page' in the school magazine, *The Hightown Herald*.

"I've got an advance copy of the next magazine!" Kim said, diving into her bag and pulling it out. Although she hadn't been doing the column for very long, she was enjoying it enormously, and it was all good practice for when she became an animal trainer herself. "Take a look!"

Sarah took the copy of *The Hightown Herald* and flipped through it until she came to Kim's column. Kim's Animal Problem Page was emblazoned across the top of the page in bright red and gold letters, and underneath it said: Have you got a problem with your pet? Is your cat driving you crazy? Is your dog doing daft things? Let Kim help you sort it out!

"I've had about fifteen letters for the next magazine," Kim said. "I thought I'd make a start on answering them while we're hanging around on the set."

"What sort of problems have you had so far?" Sarah asked curiously.

"Lucy Simpson in Year 3 has got a cat called Sooty who won't use the catflap!" Kim told her. "She wants to know if I can help her train it."

Sarah looked interested. "So what are you going to tell her?" she began, but then she stopped. "Look, what's going on over there?"

Kim squinted across the playground. A whole crowd of children was gathered in the corner, and in the middle of them was Charlotte Appleby, who was also in Miss Walker's class.

Kim groaned. "What's Charlotte up to now?"

"Let's go and find out," Sarah suggested.

Kim pulled a face. "Do we have to? Charlotte Appleby makes me want to throw up – and I've only just had my breakfast!" Kim had never liked Charlotte ever since the other girl had got rid of the Persian kitten her parents had given her, simply because the *Animal Stars* agency had politely refused to use it for TV work. The kitten had been rather nervous, and Kim's parents hadn't considered it suitable. Charlotte had been furious, and ever since then she had been extremely rude about *Animal Stars*.

"Come on," Sarah was already dragging Kim across the playground. "If Charlotte's making an idiot of herself, I want to know all about it!"

"– and the TV crew are coming tomorrow to film some scenes for *North Park Avenue* out in the countryside near the river!" Charlotte was announcing to the goggle-eyed crowd of children around her. She was a tall, thin girl, with long black hair swept up into a high ponytail and, as usual, her faithful but fairly dim sidekick Rosie Randall was by her side. "I don't know which actors are coming exactly, but my dad says Jamie Marshall's one of them."

Kim glanced at Sarah, and shrugged. Trust Charlotte Appleby to find out about the arrival of the TV crew before anyone else. She was a complete know-it-all.

"You mean, Jamie Marshall who plays Paul?" gasped one of the listening children.

"Are you having us on, Charlie?" asked Scott Brennan, who was also in Kim's class, in a deeply suspicious voice.

"No, I'm not!" Charlotte snapped. "My

dad knows someone who works for the local newspaper – it's going to be in the paper tonight!" Then she caught sight of Kim and Sarah on the edge of the crowd, and she smiled. It wasn't a nice smile. "Oh, *hello*, Kim," she said in a silkily sarcastic voice. "I'm surprised *you* didn't know about *North Park Avenue* filming near here tomorrow. I mean, you know *so* much about TV, don't you?"

"I did know actually," Kim said coolly. "But my mum asked me not to go round blabbing about it." She grinned triumphantly at Charlotte. "That's because Casper's going to be in it!"

"Your dog's going to be in *North Park Avenue!*" said Scott Brennan incredulously, and the whole crowd of children immediately turned and clustered round Kim and Sarah, all talking at once and asking questions. Charlotte was left behind with Rosie, and she turned bright red with anger.

"I don't think Charlotte's too happy!" Sarah whispered in Kim's ear.

"She's going to be even more annoyed when she sees what a star Casper's going to be!" Kim said confidently. "Just wait and see!"

15

2

"This is so *cool*!" Sarah announced, her eyes as round as dinner-plates as she stared through the car window. "Does it *really* take all these people just to make one TV programme?"

It was early the following morning, and Kim's mother had driven them all, including Casper, out into the countryside to the place where *North Park Avenue* was filming. When they'd arrived and parked alongside the TV crew's trucks, Rachel had gone off to announce their arrival, leaving Kim and Sarah in the car with Casper, where they had a good view of everything that was going on.

Kim nodded. "Yeah, it's amazing, isn't it? You never see any of this when the programme's on the telly!"

The TV crew had set up camp not far from the river and the wide, flat, grassy valley was now a hive of activity. There were several large trucks parked round the area, one of which was used by the costume department, and another one, fitted out with mirrors and chairs, for make-up. There were all kinds of complicated bits of equipment lying around, including cameras, lights and a trolley full of sound equipment, with long cables snaking everywhere though the grass. There were people rushing about all over the place, some carrying walkie-talkies and clipboards. There was also a catering van parked at one side of the set and, next to it, a big green double-decker bus.

"What's that bus doing there?" Sarah asked in amazement.

Kim grinned. "That's the canteen," she explained, "It's got tables and chairs inside."

"And where are the actors?" Sarah asked eagerly.

"They might be in those trailers over there," Kim pointed to two large caravans parked on the side of the grassy slope. "That's kind of their private place, where they can go to relax. Or they might be getting dressed or having their make-up done."

"Tell me again who's coming?" Sarah said for the twentieth time.

"There's Jamie Marshall – that's Paul, Nicholas Stevens, who plays Paul's brother Matt, and the actress who plays their mum." Kim ticked them off on her fingers. "My mum let me have a sneaky look at the script last night – it's all about Paul and Matt going on a boating holiday with their mum."

"That must be the boat there." Sarah pointed at a brightly-painted narrowboat, moored at the riverbank near where the cameras were set up. "So what happens?"

"Well, Paul finds a stray dog," Kim told her. "That's Casper. He wants to keep it, but his mum says no and then—" She leaned over and picked up the script, which was lying on the passenger seat. "Here, take a look for yourself!"

"I think I want to be an actress when I grow

up!" Sarah sighed dreamily, as she leafed through the pages.

Kim grinned. "You have to get up really early every morning, and spend ages hanging round doing nothing," she pointed out. "And look at all those words you have to learn!"

"I don't care," Sarah said. "Anyway, Casper doesn't seem to mind!"

The two girls looked round at the retriever, who was lying sprawled out in his spacious wire cage in the back of the Millers' Volvo. Casper sat up when he saw them looking at him, and barked softly.

"Not much longer to wait, boy," Kim told him, pushing her fingers through the wire mesh. "You'll soon be out of there."

Casper rubbed his head against Kim's hand, and then stared out of the window at all the activity, his eyes bright with interest.

"He looks like he knows what's going on!" Sarah laughed. "D'you think he likes being on TV?"

"Oh, sure he does!" Kim said confidently, "Casper and Harry love it. They think it's just a big game! And anyway," she added, "Mum doesn't make them work if they're getting tired or a bit fed up."

"Will Casper be OK with all these people watching?" Sarah asked, pointing at the small but steadily-growing crowd of onlookers in the distance, who were hanging around behind the barriers the TV crew had erected. A couple of the crew with walkie-talkies were patrolling the area, and keeping an eye on them.

Kim nodded. "Casper's pretty laid back. He doesn't lose his cool easily. Anyway, I don't know why they've bothered to come and watch – they won't be allowed any closer, so they won't be able to see the actual filming. Then she groaned. "Look who's over there!"

Sarah grinned as she spotted Charlotte Appleby at the front of the crowd, right next to the barrier. "I bet she was the first one here!"

"Yeah, Rosie looks like she's still half-asleep!" Kim giggled, as Rosie Randall, who was standing next to Charlotte as usual, gave a huge yawn.

"Oh, she always looks like that!" Sarah sat up and looked out of the window. "Here's your mum."

"OK, you two," Rachel said briskly, as she opened up the back of the car, "Let's get moving. Kim, will you bring the kit bag and the script?"

Kim picked up the rucksack, which had *Animal Stars Agency* printed on the front. She always helped her mum to pack it the night before with anything they might need for a job, such as dog brushes, treats and Casper's favourite toys.

"Come on, Casper." Kim's mother unlocked the retriever's cage, and let him jump out on to the grass. Casper gave his shaggy coat a good shake, and then sniffed the air with interest. "We've got to get you into make-up."

"Casper has to wear *make-up*?" Sarah asked, her eyes wide.

"Sort of," Kim's mother said with a smile, "Casper's supposed to be a stray dog, so he's got to be made-up to look like one."

"Can they do that?" Sarah asked doubtfully, looking at Casper's gleaming golden coat.

"Yeah, they use hair gel and dark hair dye to make his coat look all scruffy," Kim explained.

"Cool!" Sarah exclaimed with a grin. Then suddenly she grabbed Kim's arm and squeezed it hard. "Look! That's – that's—"

"It's Paul's brother, Matt!" said Kim, staring at the boy who was walking down the steps of one of the trucks. He was a good few years older than

Kim and Sarah, and he was already in costume, wearing his usual black leather jacket and ripped jeans. His dark hair was slicked back with gel, and he had a gold ring through one nostril. "I mean, it's Nicholas Stevens, who plays Matt."

"He looks a bit rough, doesn't he?" Sarah said nervously. "D'you think he's like Matt in real life?"

"I hope not," Kim whispered with a grin. "Remember when he tried to mug that old lady?"

"Yes, and he got caught shoplifting!" Sarah added under her breath.

"*And* he's the leader of that gang who keep breaking into houses!" Kim reminded her.

"Look! He's coming over to us!" Sarah squeaked, sounding alarmed.

"Relax, Sarah," said Kim's mother, "I'm sure Nicholas is nothing like Matt!"

"Hiya," said Nicholas with a friendly smile, as he came up to them. "I'm Nick Stevens. I play Matt Cooper in the show."

"Nice to meet you, Nick." Kim's mother introduced herself and the girls. Kim managed to say hello, but Sarah was completely tongue-tied, and Kim had to elbow her in the ribs.

"Er – um – hello!" Sarah muttered in a shaky

voice, staring at Nick Stevens as if he'd hypnotised her. "Have you *really* had your nose pierced?"

"Sarah!" Kim hissed, but Nick just laughed.

"You must be kidding!" He pulled the nose-ring out, and showed it to them. "It's just a clip-on job. I'm too much of a coward to have it done for real!"

"And you've already met Casper, of course," Kim's mum said, as Nick carefully put the ring back in his nose.

"I sure have. Hi, Casper." Nick squatted down to pat the dog on the head, then laughed as Casper solemnly raised his paw. "You want to shake hands, do you? OK!"

"He likes you!" Kim said, delighted.

Nick looked pleased. "Great. I love dogs."

Kim and Sarah glanced at each other. As far as they could tell, Nick was *nothing* like Matt!

"Look after Casper for me, will you, Kim?" asked her mother, handing her the lead. "I must go and have a word with Tony, the director, before we go to make-up."

"Watch it," Nick told her, "He's in a bit of a bad mood at the moment. But then he's *always* in a bad mood!"

"Most directors usually are!" said Kim's mother dryly, and went off.

"Where are the other actors?" Sarah asked Nick eagerly.

"Still in make-up," Nick replied, "But there's not that many of the cast of *North Park Avenue* here anyway. Just me, Jamie Marshall and Sally Lewis – she plays our mum."

"What about your baby sister?" Kim asked. "Your baby sister in the programme, I mean?"

Nick shook his head. "No, the twins aren't here."

"The *twins*?" Sarah looked puzzled.

"Yeah, our little sister's played by identical twins," Nick told her.

"Why?" Sarah wanted to know.

"Well, if one's playing up and screaming her head off, the other one can do the filming instead," Nick explained.

Sarah's eyes opened wide. "Making a TV programme is loads more complicated than I thought it would be." Then she stopped, and clutched Kim's arm. "Look, Kim! Over there!"

A boy with a familiar shock of white-blond hair was sauntering down the steps of the trailer Nick himself had just come out of. Kim and Sarah stared at him, their eyes wide.

"It's Jamie Marshall!" Kim said breathlessly. She didn't get excited about meeting TV stars very often because she'd seen so many, but Jamie Marshall was one of her big favourites.

"Yeah, that's Jamie . . ." Nick said in a rather acid voice. Kim glanced at him, surprised. She wondered if Nick was jealous because Jamie was so popular. That must be why he looked like he'd swallowed a lemon.

Jamie glanced round casually, then spotted Nick standing with Kim, Sarah and Casper. He waved, and headed over in their direction.

"He's coming over here!" Sarah gabbled in Kim's ear. "Oh, I think I'm going to DIE if he speaks to me!"

"Hi." Jamie walked up to them, smiling the angelic smile which had made him the darling of mums and grannies all over the country. "I'm Jamie Marshall."

"Hello," Kim stammered, while Sarah couldn't even manage that. She simply stared at Jamie with her mouth open.

"And I've already met Casper." Jamie knelt

down, and stroked the dog's head, and Casper wagged his tail happily. "I reckon we're going to be great mates, aren't we, boy?" He felt in the pocket of his jeans, then looked up at Kim. "Is it OK to give him a dog biscuit?"

"Jamie, I don't think you ought to do that," Nick Stevens said in a warning voice.

"No, it's all right," Kim said with a smile, desperately hoping that her mum would let her get Jamie's autograph before filming finished. She

26

wasn't usually allowed to ask, but this was *Jamie Marshall*.

Jamie held out the biscuit to Casper, who sniffed it first, and then took hold of it eagerly. A second or two later, though, the retriever began to cough and splutter.

"Casper!" Kim said, alarmed. "What's wrong?"

Shaking his head in distress, Casper spat the biscuit out on to the grass, and Jamie Marshall burst out laughing.

"Got you, you stupid mutt!" he said gleefully, and then sauntered away, still laughing his head off.

3

"I still can't believe what that Jamie Marshall did to Casper," Kim muttered grimly to Sarah for about the millionth time. "Luke was right – Jamie's *nothing* like Paul!"

"He's gross!" Sarah agreed indignantly. "Fancy giving poor old Casper a trick dog biscuit!"

"I wonder if he's planning to play any more jokes," Kim said in a worried voice. She glanced across the set at Jamie Marshall, who was now on his best behaviour, chatting to Kim's mum and stroking Casper, along with Nick Stevens. Kim hadn't had a chance yet to get her mum on her own, and tell her what had happened. "I just don't trust him."

"I don't think Nick likes him very much either," Sarah remarked.

Kim shrugged. "I bet Jamie's played tricks on him too, that's why!"

"Right, clear the set please," called one of the assistant directors, Rob Kennedy, a red-headed man with glasses. "We're starting with Scene Four, as per your shooting schedule. Jamie and the dog on set, please."

Sarah looked anxiously at Kim. "Jamie's going to be acting with Casper right now! D'you think he'll behave himself? Jamie, I mean, not Casper!"

"I don't know," Kim said in a worried voice, "I think I'd better try and warn my mum what Jamie's like."

"Yeah, that might be a good idea." Nick Stevens came up to them at that moment, a sober look on his face. "Once Jamie gets going, there's no telling what he might do!"

"Is he always like this then?" Kim asked in dismay.

Nick nodded. "Oh, yeah. He always carries loads of those stupid tricks around with him!" He shrugged. "I think all the fame's gone to his head. He used to be OK when we first started working together."

"Has he ever played any jokes on you?" Sarah said.

"You bet," Nick replied grimly. "Once he swapped my hair gel for some joke stuff – it turned my hair bright green!"

"What happened?" Sarah gasped.

"Oh, it washed out – eventually!" Nick said with a grin, "But it held up the filming, and Liam, who was our director then, threw a fit."

"So Jamie got into trouble?" Kim asked hopefully.

Nick hesitated. "Well, not really . . . He's so popular with the viewers that he gets away with murder! And he's clever too."

"What do you mean?" Sarah said.

"Well, it's not always obvious that he's to blame, and, anyway, he doesn't play tricks on important people like the producer and the director. He usually picks on people who won't bother to complain – you know, actors who are maybe appearing in only one or two episodes."

"Like Casper," Kim said grimly.

Nick nodded. "I keep hoping the scriptwriters of *North Park Avenue* might decide to kill Paul off," he admitted, "but no such luck yet!"

"D'you think Jamie might try to put Casper off while they're actually filming?" Kim asked nervously.

"He might," Nick said slowly. "But if he does, you can bet he'll be clever about it."

"Are Jamie's mum or dad here?" Kim wanted to know. "Maybe they could do something."

"Jamie's mum sometimes comes with him," Nick replied, "But she's not here at the moment."

"Well, don't you and Jamie have a tutor or something?" Sarah asked, "Couldn't they sort Jamie out?"

"Yeah, Mrs Jennings. That's her over there." Nick pointed out a short, plump woman who was buying a cup of coffee at the catering van. "She kind of looks after us while we're working. But she only started this week, so she doesn't really know what Jamie's like yet."

"What happened to the last one?" Kim asked.

Nick rolled his eyes. "She left after Jamie

superglued her handbag shut!"

"Right, that does it!" Kim said in a worried voice, "I've got to warn Mum that Jamie Marshall might be up to something!" And she hurried off.

"Hang on, Kim," Nick called after her, "They're just about to start filming!"

Kim ignored him, and hurried round the edge of the filming area to where her mother was standing, holding Casper by his collar. Rachel had to position herself carefully so that Casper could see her and hear her instructions, but so that she wasn't in the shot. The scene that was about to be filmed was the one where Paul meets the stray dog for the first time on the path along the river, and Casper's coat had been treated by the make-up department, so that it now looked scruffy and straggly.

"Mum!" Kim hissed, stopping a few feet away from where her mother was standing. "Mum, I need to talk to you!"

Her mother frowned. "Kim, we're about to start filming!" she said crossly, "This had better be important!"

"It is," Kim assured her. She knew that her mother absolutely hated being interrupted when she was getting ready to start a scene, but Kim also knew she couldn't run the risk of Casper being hurt or scared, if Jamie decided to play another trick on him.

Her mother glanced anxiously across at the director, Tony Allison, who was a short, stocky man with a shock of blond hair and a grumpy expression on his face. He was still in consultation with the man in charge of the lighting, and wasn't quite ready to start, so she hurried over to Kim, bringing Casper with her.

"What is it?" she asked shortly.

"It's Jamie, Mum!" Kim whispered. There were quite a lot of the TV crew milling around, and she didn't want them to hear what she was saying. "He's really nasty – he played a horrible trick on Casper!"

Her mum raised her eyebrows. "Kim, what are you talking about?"

"Just keep an eye on Jamie, Mum!" Kim said desperately, "He might try to do something while he and Casper are acting together!"

"We'd like to start filming now if you don't mind!" called an irritable voice, and Kim and her mother both looked up to find Rob Kennedy, the assistant director, glaring at them from the other side of the set.

Kim suddenly realised that everyone else had gone quiet. Blushing furiously, she stumbled backwards, almost tripping over a cable. Her mother threw her a look, and moved back into position with Casper. Kim knew that look. It meant "Later."

"You OK?" Nick asked in a low voice, as Kim scurried hastily back towards him and Sarah.

"I don't think Mum believed me," Kim told him. She looked up, and saw that Jamie, who was standing on the deck of the boat, was grinning smugly at her. Kim could tell that he'd guessed what she'd been saying to her mother.

"Right, we're going for a rehearsal," shouted Rob Kennedy, as Kim glared at Jamie. "Can we have silence on set *please*!"

The message was relayed on walkie-talkies to the assistant floor managers who were keeping an eye on the watching crowd, and everyone fell silent. Kim sat down on the grass again next to Sarah, and fixed her eyes grimly on Jamie Marshall. If he did *anything* to harm or annoy Casper, she was going to make sure everyone knew about it . . .

The rehearsal began. Jamie, as Paul, jumped off the boat on to the path, and began to walk along the river, towards a camera with a very long lens which was filming his every move. When Jamie reached a certain point along the path, which was marked by a plastic peg stuck in the grass, Kim's mother released her grip on Casper's collar.

"Casper – chase him!" she ordered the retriever. "Chase!" Although Rachel's instructions to the dog would be picked up by the sound equipment, they would be edited out of the final version.

Casper bounded obediently up the towpath after Paul, who spun round, alarmed, as he heard footsteps behind him.

"Casper, stop!" shouted Kim's mother, and Casper skidded to a halt, inches in front of the boy. "Put your feet up, Casper!"

Casper jumped up, putting his front paws on Paul's chest. Paul looked scared, and then slowly toppled over backwards, landing with a thump on the grass. The scene worked so well, and the look on Jamie Marshall's face was so funny, that even Kim couldn't help smiling reluctantly.

"Cut it! Great stuff, Jamie – that was perfect!" shouted Tony Allison, also managing a smile for once. "And well done – er – the dog! We'll go for a take this time."

"Jamie didn't do anything to Casper, did he?" Sarah whispered in Kim's ear.

Kim shook her head, and squirmed uncomfortably, as she saw her mother glance over at her with a frown. She watched intently as Jamie and Casper ran through the scene again, needing a couple of takes to get it absolutely right. After that, the director went on to rehearse and shoot several other scenes between Jamie and Casper, including the scene where Paul makes friends with the dog, and takes it back to the boat, but Jamie didn't put a foot wrong.

"Looks like Jamie's decided to behave himself," Kim muttered to Nick, as one of the assistant directors announced a coffee break.

"That won't last," Nick said wearily. "It never does!"

Sarah was leafing through Nick's copy of the script, looking confused. "I don't get it!" she grumbled. "They've missed out loads of scenes!"

"We don't shoot the scenes in order," Nick told her with a grin, "We're just shooting all the outside scenes with the boat for the next few days, while the weather's good. We'll do the inside shots in the cabin later."

"Oh." Sarah squinted doubtfully at the narrowboat bobbing gently up and down on the river. "That boat looks really small to film on."

"We're not filming any inside shots on that one!" Nick said, "We're using a bigger boat for the cabin scenes, so we've got more room inside."

He and Kim both burst out laughing at the look on Sarah's face.

"Nothing on TV is as it seems!" Sarah remarked

thoughtfully, "I don't think I'll be an actress after all – it looks like a lot of hard work!"

"Oh-oh, here comes The Pain!" Nick muttered with a groan. Kim looked round to see Jamie Marshall sauntering towards them carrying a glass of Coca-Cola, and smiling smugly. Kim's blood began to boil.

"What're you grinning at?" she snapped.

"Kim!" Sarah said warningly.

"You," Jamie said with a sneer. "So what're you going to do about it? Go running to tell tales to Mumsy-Wumsy again?"

Kim clenched her fists. "Yeah, I've told her what a nasty little creep you are!"

"And she doesn't believe you, right?" Jamie raised his eyebrows.

"Maybe not, but you'd better not play any more tricks on Casper, or you'll be in big trouble!" Kim snapped, wondering how on earth she could ever have been a Jamie Marshall fan.

Jamie shrugged. "Ooh, I'm terrified!" he said sarcastically. "Look, I do *what* I like *when* I like. Got it?" Then he grinned widely. "Here comes Mummy. Looks like *you're* the one in big trouble!"

Kim looked round and her heart sank. Her

mother was marching towards them with Casper trotting along patiently beside her. She didn't look very pleased.

"Kim!" she called sharply. "I want a word with you. In private!"

4

"And you're going to have to behave a bit better than that if you want to come on set with me ever again, young lady!" Kim's mother said crossly, as she pulled into the Millers' driveway. "You *know* you're not supposed to interrupt me when filming's about to start, and then you go round making up stories about Jamie Marshall!"

"I wasn't making up stories!" Kim said indignantly, "He *did* give Casper a joke dog biscuit!"

"Well, he was perfectly polite and professional when he was working with Casper and me!" her mother retorted, braking to a halt outside their house. "All right, maybe he did play a little trick on Casper, but I'm sure he won't do it again."

"He will – he's a spoilt, big-headed brat!" Kim snapped.

"Kim, shut up," Sarah muttered between her teeth, as Casper whined dismally in the back of the car. He hated it when his family got into arguments.

"Well, if you feel like that, maybe you'd better not come to the set tomorrow," Kim's mother said in an acid voice, as she turned off the engine.

Kim bit down hard on her tongue to stop herself from saying anything else. Once she and her mum started arguing, it usually led to fireworks, and being banned from the filming was the one thing she *didn't* want. Somebody had to keep an eye on Casper in case Jamie Marshall got up to his tricks again.

"Sorry," she muttered, and Sarah glanced at her, relieved.

"OK, forget it," said Kim's mother abruptly, as she let Casper out of the back of the car.

"Hello, you lot! How was *North Park Avenue?*" The front door opened, and Kim's father came out. He took one look at their gloomy faces, and did a double-take. "That bad, was it?"

"It was all right," Kim said shortly as she climbed out of the car.

Her father raised his eyebrows. "Is there something you're not telling me?"

At that moment Harry and Spike came dashing out of the house to greet them, jumping up at each person in turn, and then sniffing busily at Casper, trying to work out where he'd been all day.

"It was a bit difficult, but we got through it," Kim's mother said quickly. "How have things been here?"

"Pretty busy, actually." Kim's father looked pleased. "I think Spike may have got his first job!"

"Excellent!" Kim perked up immediately when she heard that. "What is it?"

"A TV commercial for a new brand of soft drink," her father told her. "I sent Spike's photo to the ad agency, and they loved him! They want to audition him as soon as possible."

"I didn't think Spike was properly trained yet,"

Sarah remarked, bending down to stroke the shaggy little dog who was sniffing round her feet.

"He's not fully trained like Harry or Casper, but this ad doesn't sound too demanding," Kim's father explained. "They're going to have some fantastic special effects in it too."

"Sounds good . . ." Kim's parents went into the house together, and Sarah heaved a sigh of relief.

"I thought your mum was going to say we couldn't go to the filming any more!"

"I know," Kim said grimly, "I was biting my tongue so hard, I nearly bit it in half!"

"I don't think she believes you about Jamie though," Sarah said doubtfully.

"I don't care," Kim said in a determined voice. She knelt down and put her arms round Casper's neck, and the big dog gently licked her face. "I don't care if Jamie Marshall's the most famous person on the planet, and I don't care if I get into grief with Mum. I'm not going to let Jamie play any more tricks on Casper!"

"Right, can we have the artists on set for Scene 7, please?"

"That's me." Nick Stevens grinned at Kim and

Sarah, and gave Kim his cup of tea to hold. "This is my first scene with Casper. Wish me luck!"

It was early the following morning, and everyone was back at the riverbank for the second day's filming. Kim's mum had given both girls another stern warning about their behaviour, and had made sure they were seated on the grass, well away from the cameras, before she'd taken Casper off to make-up.

"And don't move a muscle!" she'd told them, only half-joking.

Nick had come over to say hello to them, but Jamie Marshall hadn't. He was really annoying Kim though, because he kept looking over at them and grinning all over his face.

"That Jamie Marshall is a pain!" Kim muttered to Sarah, as Nick went across the set towards the boat. "He's smirking at us again!"

"Take no notice of him," Sarah told her firmly.

"No, I've got to watch him all the time!" Kim retorted. "I've got to make sure he doesn't try any of his nasty little tricks on Casper again."

"So how are you getting on with the problem page?" Sarah asked quickly, more to distract Kim than anything else.

"Here, take a look." Kim put her hand in her jacket pocket and pulled out a pile of folded letters. "I brought them with me in case I get a chance to work on them. Not much hope of that though, now I've got to watch Jamie Marshall!"

"Oh, here's Lucy's letter about her cat." Sarah pulled it out and read it. "You never did tell me how you were going to help Sooty use the catflap!"

"Well—" Kim began, and then stopped. Everyone was moving into position for filming, and she watched Jamie Marshall intently.

"Can we get a move on, please!" shouted Tony Allison, who was looking even grumpier than usual. "Where's Sally?"

"Here I am." Sally Lewis, the actress who played the boys' long-suffering mother Mrs Cooper, hurried across the set towards the boat, where Jamie and Nick were already waiting. Kim's mother was already standing on the riverbank, holding Casper by the collar.

"If we're *quite* ready then . . ." said the director sarcastically.

"Stay, Casper," Kim's mother told the retriever quietly, and then moved out of the way, so that she wouldn't be caught on film. Casper sat down immediately at Jamie's feet, wagging his tail slowly from side to side. Her heart pounding with nerves, Kim watched closely, but Jamie wasn't taking any notice of Casper at all.

"OK – action!" called the assistant director. There was silence for a second or two, and then the scene began.

"Oh, Mum *why* can't I keep him?" Paul said, stroking the dog's head, "He doesn't belong to anybody, and he's a brilliant dog."

"Paul, we just can't afford it," said Mrs Cooper helplessly.

"Yeah, what do we want a stupid mutt like that for!" Matt sneered, glaring at the dog.

"Casper," Kim's mother said in a low voice from the sidelines, "Speak." Casper immediately gave a low, warning bark, deep in his throat. Matt took a step backwards, looking alarmed.

"Hey, did you hear that? That mangy old mutt's gonna attack me!"

"No, he isn't!" Paul said quickly.

"You'd better take him back to where you found him, Paul—" his mother began.

Paul stared at her unhappily, his lips trembling. Then he turned and ran off down the path.

"Casper, chase him!" Kim's mother told the retriever, pointing at Jamie, and Casper galloped off after him.

"Cut it!" called the director, "Can we run through that again? Jamie, there'll be a close-up on you at the end, so can we have some tears in your eyes?"

"No problem," Jamie said jauntily, as a make-up girl hurried over to comb his hair back into place and apply caustic stick under his eyes.

"I could pull his hair for him," Kim said in a low voice to Sarah, "That'd bring tears to his eyes!"

"Sssh!" Sarah giggled. "Someone might hear!"

After a few more takes, the scene was filmed to the director's satisfaction. Once again, Jamie behaved himself, and Kim began to wonder if she was worrying about nothing. Jamie didn't seem to have any other tricks up his sleeve. On the other hand, he might just be waiting for the right moment . . .

The next scene which Casper was involved in was a rather dramatic one. Matt was on the boat deck, trying to steal some money from his mother's purse, while she and Jamie were down in the cabin. Unfortunately for Matt, Casper was watching him, and, growling, backed Matt into a corner and made him drop the handbag. The scene between Nick and Casper worked so well, it was filmed in only two takes.

"Casper's a really brilliant actor!" Nick said when the scene was over, and it was time for a coffee break. "He's better than some of the others I have to work with!"

"I think I know who you mean!" Kim said, pulling a face at Jamie Marshall's back as he went into one of the trailers. "Still, at least he hasn't done anything since yesterday."

"No . . ." Nick said hesitantly. "But usually when Jamie's on his best behaviour, it means he's got something mega planned!"

Kim groaned. "I can't believe I was looking forward to coming to the filming – now I can't wait for it to be over, so I'll won't have to worry about Jamie's next trick!"

"He's got a long scene coming up with Casper next," Nick said with a frown, glancing at his copy of the script. "Maybe he's got something sorted for that."

"If he puts Casper off when they're supposed to

be filming, my mum might get blamed," Kim said, looking worried.

"We'll just have to wait and see," Sarah told her, "there's no point in trying to warn your mum – she won't believe you."

Kim nodded. As soon as Jamie came out of the trailer again and went over to the catering van, she fixed her eyes on him like a hawk, and watched his every move. But Jamie didn't do anything suspicious. It was only when the assistant director called for Jamie and Casper to get ready on set to rehearse their next scene, that Kim noticed anything unusual. Then she nudged Sarah and Nick, who were sitting either side of her.

"Look at Jamie!"

"Why? What's he doing?" Sarah asked.

"He keeps putting his hand in his pocket!" Kim hissed.

"So? It's not a crime, is it?" Nick pointed out with a grin.

"I reckon he's got something in there!" Kim said in a determined voice. "Something he's going to use to play a trick on Casper!"

They all watched silently as Jamie and Casper

moved into position. The scene was a simple one, involving Paul and the dog walking along the riverbank, and Kim didn't see what could possibly go wrong. But knowing Jamie Marshall, it was quite likely that something might.

"Don't take your eyes off him!" she whispered to Nick and Sarah, as the rehearsal began.

"I don't know what we're going to do, boy," Paul whispered, as he and Casper walked slowly along the riverbank, towards the camera, Kim's mother watching them just out of shot. "My mum won't let me keep you. I wish she would. I really

need a friend to talk to sometimes . . ."

Kim pulled a face at Sarah. She could just imagine all the mums and grannies all over the country going "Aaah!" when they saw this on TV.

"Things are a bit difficult at home," Paul went on, "My brother's got in with this gang, and they've got him stealing and doing burglaries. . ." He took his hand out of his pocket, and stroked the dog's nose. "I wish my dad still lived with us – hey, what's going on!"

Jamie leapt backwards rapidly as Casper suddenly began to sneeze violently, three or four

times in quick succession, shaking his shaggy head from side to side in distress.

"Cut!" yelled the assistant director furiously. "What on earth's the matter with the dog?"

"I don't know." Kim's mother rushed up to Casper, and tried to take the retriever's head in her hands so she could look closely at him. But Casper was still sneezing loudly and coughing, and he pulled away from her.

"Maybe he's ill," Jamie suggested helpfully.

"Ill!" Tony Allison glared at Kim's mother. "I'm not paying you to have a sick dog on set!"

"Casper's not ill," Kim's mother said, keeping her temper with difficulty. "I'm not sure what's the matter with him."

"Well, sort it out then!" the director snapped, "You've got five minutes – and I *mean* five minutes!"

As her mother led Casper, still sneezing, away, Kim turned to Nick and Sarah. "I *told* you!" she said fiercely. "Jamie Marshall had something in his pocket which made Casper sneeze – and that little creep's not going to get away with it this time!"

5

"Kim, wait!" Sarah called as Kim jumped to her feet, and headed off in Jamie's direction. But Kim ignored her. She was furious. Jamie Marshall had no right to make Casper suffer – and if he kept on playing tricks like that, the director would get fed up and blame the dog and Kim's mother. Tony Allison might even *sack* Casper, and that wouldn't be good for *Animal Stars* . . .

"Hold on a minute," Kim caught up with Jamie just as he reached the trailer he shared with Nick. "I want a word with you!"

"Oh, not you again." Jamie paused, and yawned rudely. "I think I'll get Tony to throw you off the set!"

"Go on then." Kim put her hands on her hips, and stared hard at him. "If you do, I'll tell him what you did to Casper!"

Jamie shrugged. "I didn't do anything. I can't help it if your stupid dog's ill, can I?"

"Casper's not stupid, and he's *not* ill!" Kim hissed furiously, as Sarah and Nick hurried over to join them. "*You* made him sneeze like that!"

"Me!" Jamie raised his eyebrows in a very annoying manner. "How did I do that then?"

Kim was now so angry, she couldn't stop herself. Instead of saying anything, she simply lunged forward, and grabbed at Jamie's pocket.

"Kim, what are you doing!" Sarah squealed anxiously.

Jamie wasn't expecting Kim to fly at him like that, and he was taken unawares. Kim managed to get her hand into his jacket pocket before Jamie could stop her, and she pulled out a small, open packet.

" 'Pepper Dust'!" she read out triumphantly.

" 'Make your friends and family sneeze their heads off with Perkins' Pepper Dust – now twice as strong!' " She showed the packet to Nick and Sarah. "That's what you used to make Casper sneeze!"

"I did not!" Jamie spluttered furiously.

"Oh, come off it, Jamie," said Nick, "why don't you just admit it?"

Jamie shrugged sulkily. "It was only a bit of a laugh," he muttered.

"A bit of a laugh!" Kim repeated angrily. "You could have got Casper the sack!"

"So?" Jamie shrugged again. "Who cares?"

Kim glared at him, unable to believe her ears. "You've got to be the most horrible person I've ever met in my whole life!" Forgetting that the packet was open, Kim threw it furiously back at Jamie. "Here, take your stupid Pepper Dust!"

"What d'you think you're doing!" Jamie spluttered, as a cloud of fine black powder flew out of the packet and enveloped him. "A-tishoo!"

"Serves you right," Kim told him, retreating to a safe distance along with Nick and Sarah, "now you know what poor Casper felt like!"

"A-tishoo! I'll – a-tishoo! – get you for this!"

Jamie snapped, rubbing his watery eyes. "A-tishoo!"

"What on earth's going on here?" asked a stern voice behind them. "Jamie, are you all right?"

Kim looked round. It was Mrs Jennings, Nick and Jamie's tutor, and she was staring suspiciously at them. Kim glanced at Sarah and Nick and bit her lip, already regretting what she'd done. If Jamie complained about her, he could certainly get her thrown off the set. Then she wouldn't be around to try and protect Casper, and, *boy*, would her mother be mad ... She might even ban Kim from going out on jobs with her in future.

Her heart in her mouth, Kim looked at Jamie. What would he say? Surely he'd grab this opportunity to get her into trouble?

"*I said*, what's going on here?" Mrs Jennings repeated more sharply. "Jamie, are you ill?"

Jamie had stopped sneezing by now, and the packet of Pepper Dust had disappeared back into his pocket. "No, I'm fine, Mrs Jennings." He gave Kim a challenging look. "I'm just talking to my *friends* here."

Kim felt her knees wobble with relief. Jamie couldn't really complain about Kim without giving himself away, now that the Pepper Dust was back in his pocket. It looked like she was safe.

"Kim, you shouldn't have done that!" Sarah said anxiously, as Mrs Jennings, still looking suspicious, accompanied Jamie into the trailer. "You could've got into real trouble!"

"Yeah, I thought Jamie was going to blow a fuse when you chucked that pepper stuff at him!" Nick chuckled.

"I know I shouldn't have done it, but he really makes me lose my cool," Kim admitted. "I thought he was going to drop me right in it too, but he didn't."

"Yeah, but I reckon it's war now," Nick said slowly.

"What do you mean?" Kim asked.

"Well, all Jamie's got to do is say the word, and you could be banned from the set," Nick explained soberly. "But he hasn't done that. That means he's got something else in mind . . ."

Kim groaned. "You mean, he's going to carry on trying to wind me up by playing tricks on Casper?"

Nick nodded. "Yeah, I reckon he's really hacked off because you've been standing up to him. Most people just keep quiet and put up with it."

"So I've just made things worse," Kim muttered, wishing for the millionth time that she could learn to control her temper. "But I was worried about Casper, that's all."

"It's not your fault," Nick assured her. "Jamie's definitely to blame."

"I think I'd better go and tell Mum what's happened," Kim sighed. "At least then she can keep an eye on Jamie."

Sarah and Nick both looked doubtful. "D'you think she'll believe you?" Nick asked.

"She might," Kim said, looking doubtful herself.

"I mean, she knows *something* must've happened to make Casper sneeze."

"Right, can we have Jamie and Casper back on set for Scene 14 please?" shouted the assistant director.

"If the dog's up to it," added Tony Allison with a scowl.

"He's fine," Kim's mother said calmly from where she was standing with Casper on the side of the set. Kim knew that her mother was probably really angry inside, but she hardly ever lost her cool when she was working. Kim also knew that if she was ever going to be a successful animal trainer, she was going to have to learn to control her temper too. She didn't quite know how though – especially when she was face to face with an annoying, big-headed brat like Jamie Marshall.

"Where's Jamie?" Tony Allison called irritably from his chair on the side of the set. "We've wasted enough time this morning."

Jamie dashed across the grass and in front of the cameras. He had obviously been in the middle of eating something because he was still chewing.

"Oh, take your time and finish what you're eating, why don't you," grumbled the director sarcastically. "We've only wasted half the morning already!"

Jamie didn't answer. He simply pointed at his mouth, and chewed frantically. Tony Allison rolled his eyes heavenwards, and sighed.

"What's the matter, Jamie?"

Jamie shook his head, and pointed to his mouth again. He was rapidly turning bright pink in the face.

"Why isn't he saying anything?" Tony asked irritably. "Can somebody please find out what's the matter with him?"

"Jamie?" Mrs Jennings, the boys' tutor, called from the side of the set. "Are you all right?"

"Mm-uh!" Jamie said through gritted teeth. "Uh – mmm!"

Kim, Sarah and Nick stared at each other, puzzled. What on earth was going on?

"Er – I think his teeth are stuck together!" Mrs Jennings announced to the director.

Tony Allison's mouth fell open. "Are you having me on?"

Mrs Jennings shook her head. "No, he can't open his mouth. Look!"

"That's got to be an improvement," muttered

60

one of the crew who was standing near Kim. "Let's hope it lasts!"

Everyone stared at Jamie, who was pulling his face into fantastic contortions, trying to open his mouth.

"What's he up to?" Kim whispered suspiciously to Nick and Sarah.

"Do you think we should call a doctor?" Mrs Jennings asked anxiously.

"He's trying to tell us something," one of the assistant directors said. "Give him a pencil and paper."

Everyone watched as Jamie was handed a pen and paper, and began to scribble furiously. Then he handed the paper to Mrs Jennings.

"What does it say?" Tony Allison demanded.

"It says 'Someone gave me a toffee, and it's stuck my teeth together!' " Mrs Jennings read out.

"I've got a dog who can't stop sneezing, and an actor who can't speak!" Tony Allison roared. "I'm working with a bunch of amateurs! Right, Sally and Nick, I want to talk to you about scenes for this afternoon. The rest of you, take a break while Jamie unsticks himself!"

Kim and Sarah began to giggle as Mrs Jennings led Jamie away, still trying frantically to pull his teeth apart.

"What a prat!" Kim said, "You know what? I reckon he ate one of his own joke sweets by mistake!"

"Yeah, that's probably it," Nick agreed, "Good job he didn't give one of them to Casper!"

Kim stopped laughing immediately. "I bet that's what he was planning to do!" she gasped, imagining how distressed and scared poor Casper would have been if it had been *his* teeth that were stuck together.

"I've got to go." Nick jumped to his feet. "Tony looks like he's going to have a major fit if something doesn't start going right soon!"

"That just serves Jamie Marshall right!" Sarah said with satisfaction as Nick hurried off. "I hope his mouth stays glued shut for the rest of the day!"

"How about for the rest of his life?" Kim suggested, and they started to giggle.

"What're you two laughing at?" Kim's mother asked, as she came over to them along with Casper. "Not poor Jamie Marshall, I hope?"

Kim and Sarah looked at each other.

"Well, it *did* serve him right, Mum," Kim muttered.

Her mother looked at her suspiciously.

"Kim, you didn't have anything to do with what just happened, did you? Because if you did—"

"*'Course* I didn't, Mum!" Kim interrupted indignantly. "But Jamie's been a right pain in the neck, honest!" She was just about to launch into an explanation of how Jamie had made Casper sneeze with the pepper dust, when Mrs Jennings hurried over to them.

"Mrs Miller, can I have a word?" she asked in an icy voice.

Kim's mother looked rather surprised. "Yes, of course. What about?"

"I've just managed to get poor Jamie's teeth unstuck," Mrs Jennings snapped, "And I asked him who gave him that joke toffee. He didn't want to tell me, but I kept on till he did." Her eyes swivelled round and came to rest on Kim. "He says it was your daughter!"

"*Me!*" Kim gasped, her heart beginning to pound, "I didn't give him anything!"

"Are you sure, Kim?" Her mother stared at her sternly. "You and Jamie haven't exactly been

63

getting on very well, have you?"

"Mum, it wasn't me!" Kim was so shocked, she could hardly get the words out. "It's Jamie who's always playing jokes – I bet those sweets are his!"

"Oh, don't be silly," said Mrs Jennings coldly, "why would Jamie eat one of his own trick sweets?"

"To get me into trouble!" Kim retorted angrily. "That's why he's done it!"

"Jamie said you had a whole packet of them in your bag." Mrs Jennings glanced suspiciously at the *Animal Stars* rucksack which lay on the ground at Kim's feet.

"Well, he's a big fat liar then!" Kim grabbed the rucksack, and flipped the top open. Then she held it out so that Mrs Jennings could see inside. "I haven't got any of those sweets – see for yourself!"

Mrs Jennings peered inside the rucksack. Then she put her hand in, and pulled out a small packet.

" 'Tongue-Twister Toffees' ," she read out in a freezing voice. " 'Scare your friends silly as you stick their teeth together! Guaranteed to work for at least five minutes' . . ."

6

Kim stared at the packet of Tongue-Twister Toffees with her mouth open. She was so shocked and so angry, she simply couldn't say a word.

"Kim, what on earth do you think you're playing at!" her mother said in a furious voice, as Casper whined unhappily, and pawed at the ground, looking anxiously from one to the other. "How *could* you!"

"Mum, I didn't do anything!" Kim stammered. "Those sweets aren't mine!"

"Mrs Miller, I think you and I had better have a little chat and sort this out between ourselves," Mrs Jennings said with a frown. "We don't want to involve the director or any of the rest of the crew, do we?"

"No," Kim's mother said, sounding relieved. She looked at Kim and Sarah. "Wait here and don't move a single millimetre," she snapped, handing Casper's lead to Kim. "I mean it. Don't move."

"Did – did Jamie put that packet of sweets in the rucksack, then?" Sarah asked in a trembly voice as Kim's mother and Mrs Jennings went off together.

"Yeah, he must have done. The bag's been lying around all morning . . ." Kim's knees were shaking so much, she had to sit down on the grass. She put her arms round Casper, and buried her face in the dog's warm fur. She'd never seen her mother look quite so angry before. Kim's heart sank right down into her shoes as she realised that this might be the very last time she was allowed to go out on jobs with her mother, unless she could convince her that she hadn't played that trick on Jamie Marshall . . .

"What do you think your mum's going to do?" Sarah asked anxiously.

"What, apart from kill me, you mean?" Kim rested her head against Casper's, feeling more miserable than she'd ever felt in her whole life. "She's going to go *ballistic*."

"But if you tell her what Jamie's been up to—" Sarah began.

"Yeah, I can tell her about the pepper dust and all that," Kim broke in impatiently, "But she might still think I gave Jamie that toffee to get my own back." She stroked Casper's head, and the retriever butted her hand gently, staring at her with anxious eyes. "Jamie Marshall's really dropped me in it this time . . ."

"He looks pretty pleased about it too," Sarah said in a low voice.

Kim glanced up sharply. Jamie was standing by the catering van, looking at them, and grinning all over his face. "Right, that's it!" she hissed, jumping to her feet, but Sarah grabbed her arm and hung on for dear life.

"No, Kim!" she gasped. "Remember what your mum said!"

Kim hesitated, then nodded. "I guess I'm

in enough trouble as it is," she muttered. She swallowed hard as she saw her mother coming back towards them, grim-faced. It didn't look good.

"Right, Mrs Jennings and I have talked things over," Kim's mother said abruptly, as she joined the two girls, "and she's agreed not to say anything to the director. Which is lucky, or we could *all* have been in serious trouble. You know how they feel about wasting time on set." She looked at Kim. "But Mrs Jennings wants you to stay away from the rest of the filming."

"But that's not fair!" Kim burst out. "I haven't done anything!"

Her mother stared hard at her for a moment, then sighed. "We'll have to talk about this later, Kim," she said. "The director wants to see me now."

"But, Mum—" Kim began desperately.

"I said *later*, Kim," her mother repeated. "Now I want you to take Casper back to the car, and stay there. As soon as I've spoken to Tony, I'm going to drive you home."

Kim's lips trembled as she watched her mother walk off. In all the time she'd been going out on *Animal Stars* jobs with her parents, she'd never once been banned from a set. She'd always been on her very best behaviour because she knew that was what her parents expected of her. Now it looked as if all those exciting times might be over for good, and all because she'd been trying to protect Casper.

"Come on," Sarah said, putting her arm round Kim's shoulders. "We'd better go."

Kim followed her in miserable silence, Casper trotting close to her side. Now they wouldn't be able to go to the night shoot that evening, and she'd really been looking forward to that. So, she knew, had Sarah. They wouldn't be able to say goodbye to Nick either, now that they weren't allowed at the filming any more. And worst of all, she wouldn't be able to keep an eye on Casper, to make sure that Jamie didn't get up to any of his old tricks.

"Oh well," Sarah went on, trying to sound cheerful, "at least you'll have plenty of time to work on your problem page now! We could do that while we're waiting for your mum." Kim didn't answer. She didn't cry very often, but now she was struggling not to burst into tears. It just wasn't *fair*.

It was a chilly day, so there weren't as many people standing at the barriers, especially as they'd realised that they wouldn't be allowed close enough to see any of the filming. But Kim was dismayed to see that Charlotte Appleby and her mate Rosie Randall were there again. There'd been so much happening over the last day or two, she'd forgotten all about them.

"That's all I need!" she breathed crossly in Sarah's ear.

"Look, we'll keep right away from them, OK?" said Sarah, who'd already noticed the look of triumph on Charlotte's face, and didn't like it at all.

"So what're you two doing here?" Charlotte asked gleefully, "I thought you were allowed to go on to the set."

"We changed our minds," Sarah said quickly, as Kim stared miserably at Charlotte. "We're going home instead."

"D'you know what I reckon, Rosie?" Charlotte nudged her mate. "I reckon they've done something naughty, and they've been thrown out!"

"Why don't you mind your own business—" Kim began hotly, but Sarah grabbed her arm and dragged her off towards the Millers' car.

"What did you do that for?" Kim grumbled, "I was just about to tell Charlotte what I thought of her!"

"I know," Sarah said, "That's why I dragged you away!"

Kim forced a reluctant smile. "OK, I know I've got a big mouth! But I don't need Charlotte going on at me at the moment." She sighed. "I feel bad enough as it is."

"Just wait until you've had a chance to talk to your mum," Sarah told her, "I'm sure she'll believe you. Come on, let's talk about something else. Tell me how you're going to get Sooty to use the cat flap!"

"Well—" Kim began, but just then a loud squeal from Rosie Randall made them look round.

"Look, Charlie! It's him! It's Jamie Marshall!"

"Oh, no, I don't believe it!" Kim groaned as she saw Jamie heading towards the crowd, smiling and waving. "I can't get away from him!"

"Right, we have a break in the filming, and Jamie Marshall's coming over to sign some autographs," announced one of the floor managers who was policing the crowd. "Just be patient, and

I'm sure he'll do his best to sign as many as he can."

"If he says anything to me, just hold me back!" Kim muttered, putting her arm round Casper's neck for moral support.

"Just don't let him wind you up – please!" Sarah said imploringly.

Jamie hurried forward, smiling his most charming smile, and began signing autographs by the dozen. Kim watched him, wondering how he could sometimes seem so nice, and at other times be so awful. She knew very well that there was no reason why actors and actresses should be like the characters they played on TV, but she'd never dreamt that Jamie Marshall could be so different from Paul . . .

"Can you put 'To Charlotte with lots of love from Jamie Marshall', please?" Charlotte asked breathlessly, as Jamie took her leather-bound autograph book.

"Sure," Jamie said with a dazzling smile.

"Charlotte's fluttering her eyelashes so hard, it's a wonder she doesn't knock him over!" Sarah whispered in Kim's ear, and Kim couldn't help smiling faintly.

"How's the filming going?" Charlotte asked, as Jamie signed his name in her book with a flourish.

"Oh, all right." Jamie frowned. "Although *someone* played a little trick on me, I'm afraid."

"What!" Charlotte's eyes almost popped out of her head. "Who?"

"I don't want to say," Jamie said, turning his head to stare straight at Kim. So did everyone else in the crowd, including Charlotte and Rosie.

"Yeah, *this person* gave me one of those joke toffees that glue your teeth together," Jamie went on. "It was a pretty dumb thing to do really."

The crowd of people standing around who were all listening to this, began to mutter in low voices, and to throw disapproving glances at Kim. Kim felt herself turn bright red. She opened her mouth, this time to tell Charlotte *and* Jamie what she thought of them, but a warning glance from Sarah made her close it reluctantly. She knew she couldn't afford to get into any more grief with her mother.

"That's terrible!" Charlotte exclaimed, enjoying herself no end, "I hope she got into trouble!"

"She's been banned from the set," Jamie told her with satisfaction. "I'm glad really. I'm finding it difficult enough working with that dog—" he nodded at Casper, who was sitting silently and patiently next to Kim and Sarah, "– I don't think it's properly trained!"

Everyone who was listening immediately stared curiously at Casper, and Kim almost exploded with fury. Whatever Jamie said about her, he had no right to make up stories about Casper, who was always beautifully behaved.

"My dad knows someone who works for the local newspaper," Charlotte went on eagerly, "maybe you could give them an interview."

"I might just do that." Jamie glanced sideways at Kim with a gleeful grin. "I've got plenty to tell them!"

Kim looked at Sarah, her face full of dismay. Things were going from very bad to even worse. If Jamie told the newspapers that Casper wasn't properly trained, that could be extremely bad for the *Animal Stars* agency.

"You're so lucky to be on TV, Jamie!" Charlotte gushed, as Jamie scribbled an autograph for Rosie. "I'd love to be an actress."

"Really?" Jamie said airily. "Well, stick around – I might be able to get you a part as an extra."

"An extra what?" Rosie asked, puzzled, then added "*Ow!*" as Charlotte elbowed her in the ribs.

"Jamie," called the floor manager as a message crackled through on his walkie-talkie, "your tutor says you've got to go for lunch."

"OK." Jamie handed Rosie her autograph book, and waved at his fans. "See you later, folks!"

"Oh, isn't he *lovely*!" said one adoring old lady, who was standing in the crowd.

"No, he isn't," Kim muttered under her breath, but so low that only Sarah could hear her. She was really worried about what Jamie might do next. If he started giving interviews to the newspapers complaining about Casper not being properly trained, that would be a disaster. She couldn't let Jamie get away with this. She just couldn't.

"Jamie Marshall is a *seriously* nasty little scumbag!" Sarah announced, her face pink with anger. "How can he say all those things about Casper? Casper's a better actor than he'll ever be!"

Casper gave a little bark, and solemnly presented Sarah with his paw.

"I know," Kim said in a determined voice. "That's why we've got to make sure he doesn't get away with this! And I've got a brilliant idea . . ."

7

"Whenever you say you've got a brilliant idea, I just *know* it's something that's going to get us into mega trouble!" Sarah groaned, as she, Kim and Casper walked back across the grass towards the set. "Kim, I don't think we should be doing this—"

"Look, it's pretty safe at the moment," Kim told her in a low voice, even though she knew they were taking a big risk. It was worth it, though, for Casper's sake. "There's hardly anyone around."

Because it was lunchtime, most of the crew were

either queuing up at the catering van for food, or were already sitting on the canteen bus. No-one took any notice of Kim, Sarah and Casper, as they were used to seeing them around the set anyway. Kim's mother was talking to the director, over on the other side of the set, near the river, and she had her back to them. Jamie and Mrs Jennings were nowhere to be seen. Kim hoped they were on the canteen bus, having their lunch, otherwise her plan was never going to work.

"Did you see Charlotte's face when she saw us come back on to the set?" she said. "I though she was going to have a fit!"

"I hope she doesn't tell those men with the walkie talkies that Mrs Jennings has banned us!" Sarah whispered, glancing nervously over her shoulder as if she expected someone to come running over and grab them.

"They won't take any notice of her," Kim replied, rather more confidently than she felt. "Come on!"

She led Sarah and Casper quickly round the edge of the filming area, and over to the actors' trailers. The door of the one which was being used by Jamie and Nick stood wide open.

"How do we know there's no-one in there?" Sarah asked with a frown.

"We don't," Kim answered, hoping desperately that the trailer was empty. "We'll just have to risk it."

Sarah turned pale.

"Look, you don't have to come in with me," Kim told her, "you and Casper can go back to the car."

"Don't be stupid." Sarah shook her head bravely. "Let's get on with it."

Kim risked a quick glance over her shoulder. No-one was taking any notice of them whatsoever, and her mum was still talking to Tony Allison.

"Come on, Casper," she muttered. She led the dog up the steps, and peered through the open door into the trailer. "There's no-one here!" she told Sarah with a sigh of relief.

Next second all three of them were inside the trailer, and Kim carefully pushed the door closed a little. The trailer was just like an ordinary caravan inside but bigger. It had a comfy living-room at one end, a kitchen and a lavatory and a bedroom. There were books, comics and board games lying around, and a TV in one corner, presumably to entertain Nick and Jamie when they weren't filming.

"What now?" Sarah whispered, her hair almost standing on end with fright.

"We look around," Kim told her. "Nick said Jamie always brings a whole load of jokes with him, and he must have hidden them somewhere if Mrs Jennings doesn't know anything about them. If we can find them, then we can prove to Mrs Jennings and to Mum that he's behind all this!"

"OK," Sarah agreed nervously.

They began to search the trailer, helped by Casper, who was sniffing everything with interest. Kim started in the living-room, while Sarah looked in the kitchen cupboards.

"Nothing here," Sarah muttered. "I'll try the bedroom . . ."

It only took a few minutes to search the trailer, because there weren't many places to hide things. But there was no sign of Jamie Marshall's bag of tricks.

"I don't get it!" Kim frowned. "It's got to be here *somewhere*."

"Maybe we can get Nick to help us," Sarah suggested.

Casper in the Spotlight

Before Kim could reply, both girls nearly jumped right out of their skins as the door was flung wide open. Jamie Marshall burst in, his face flushed with triumph, followed by an extremely grim-looking Mrs Jennings.

"See?" Jamie declared gleefully, "I *told* you I saw them come in here!"

Kim and Sarah stared at each other in horror. Now they were *really* for it.

"I take it your mother doesn't know you're here?" Mrs Jennings asked in a freezing voice.

Kim shook her head miserably.

"I bet they were going to play another trick on me!" Jamie gasped with pretend horror. Kim could see that he was enjoying himself enormously, and she clenched her fists. They'd played right into his hands this time.

"I think we'd better go and find Mrs Miller right away," Mrs Jennings said, fixing the two girls with a steely stare, "And then we'll – what *is* that dog doing?"

Everyone looked over at Casper, who was lying on the carpet and nosing right under the divan which was against the wall. He was scrabbling and whining, trying to get at something which was pushed right underneath.

"Get that dog out of there before he damages something!" Mrs Jennings snapped.

Kim hurried over to the retriever, and knelt down to see what he was trying to get hold of. It was nothing interesting, only a large Compendium of Board Games box. Kim had seen it under the divan herself when she'd been searching the living-room.

"Come out of there, Casper," she muttered, grabbing the retriever's lead.

Casper continued to sniff at the box with interest. He lifted the lid half-off with his nose, and Kim gasped with surprise when she saw what was inside. She grabbed the box, and pulled it out.

"What on earth are you doing?" Mrs Jennings asked, surprised, as Kim put the box on the table.

Kim glanced at Jamie, who had turned a funny shade of purple.

"This is what we were looking for, Mrs Jennings!" she said in a breathless voice, as she took the lid off the box. Although it was supposed to be a Compendium of Games, there was no Snakes and Ladders, Ludo or Dominoes in it.

" 'Mr Brown's Chilli Dog Biscuits'," Mrs Jennings read out, picking up one of the packets and small boxes crammed inside, " 'Give your dog a fright – set his mouth on fire!' "

Kim and Sarah exchanged triumphant glances.

" 'Amazing Life-Like Tarantula!' " Mrs Jennings went on, emptying more of the packets out of the box, " 'Waiter, There's a Fly in my Soup – pop this realistic-looking plastic fly into your friend's cup of tea, and watch them scream! Luminous Toothpaste – makes your teeth glow in the dark!' "

"Look at Jamie's face!" Sarah whispered to Kim.

"Yeah, I bet he wishes he had a trick that would make him invisible!" Kim whispered back. She patted Casper, who was sitting next to her. "Thanks, boy," she whispered gratefully. "You're the best!" Casper barked a couple of times, looking as if he knew he'd done something clever, but he wasn't quite sure what.

"And what's this?" Mrs Jennings pushed aside a very realistic-looking plastic dog mess, and picked up a familiar packet. "More Tongue-Twister Toffees!"

"They're – they're not mine!" Jamie spluttered.

Mrs Jennings raised her eyebrows. "Oh no?"

"No, she put them there!" Jamie glared at Kim, and took a step towards her. But he soon jumped backwards again, looking alarmed as Casper stiffened and growled slightly.

At that moment the door opened again, and Kim's mother dashed in, followed closely by Nick.

"I thought I heard Casper barking," she said with a frown, which deepened as she saw Kim and Sarah. "What on *earth*'s going on?"

"I'll let your daughter explain everything," said Mrs Jennings grimly, pointing at the box of tricks lying on the table. "Meanwhile, Jamie and I are going to have a quiet word or two . . ."

"Kim, I *cannot* believe you did that!" Kim's mother paced up and down on the grass outside the trailer, almost tearing her hair out with both hands. "And after you'd been *told* to stay away from the set and to go back to the car!"

"I know, Mum," Kim muttered, "But Jamie was going to tell the newspapers that I'd played a trick on him, and that Casper wasn't properly trained—"

"You should have let me handle it!" her mother snapped. "Kim, this isn't a *game*. I'm working here, and if anything goes wrong, I won't get asked back again. We can't afford to make any mistakes."

"Sorry," Kim mumbled, "But Jamie did keep playing tricks on Casper."

Casper thumped his tail on the ground, and looked mournfully up at her.

"I suppose he did something to give Casper the sneezes?" her mother asked.

"He had pepper dust in his pocket," Sarah told her in a subdued voice.

"That little—!" Kim's mother stopped herself just in time. "Well, I can understand why you got mad, Kim, and luckily things have turned out all right, but will you *please* keep out of trouble from now on? Or—"

Her mother didn't need to finish the sentence because Kim knew what she meant. *Or you won't be allowed to come out on jobs with me any more. Ever.*

Just then the trailer door opened, and Jamie Marshall stormed out. He glared at Kim, Sarah, Casper and Mrs Miller and then stamped down the steps, with his nose in the air. Unfortunately he caught his foot on the bottom step, and nearly fell flat on his face, which rather spoiled the effect.

Scowling, he stomped off towards the catering van.

"I'm terribly sorry, Mrs Miller," Mrs Jennings said, as she followed Jamie out. "It looks like I got things all wrong. But I've spoken to Jamie, and warned him that he's got to behave himself from now on." She smiled. "And of course Kim and Sarah are welcome to stay and watch the rest of the filming."

Kim and Sarah exchanged delighted glances.

"As long as you stay right away from Jamie Marshall!" Kim's mother added sternly, as Mrs Jennings hurried off after Jamie.

"Oh, we will!" Kim promised.

"Right, everybody back on set, please, we're going for Scene 14 again with Jamie and the dog," called the assistant director, "And no toffees this time please!"

"Well, that's my lunch break gone, and I didn't even have a cup of coffee!" Kim's mum sighed. "Oh well, it'll be worth it if things go smoothly this time."

"See you later, Casper." Kim knelt down, and gave the retriever a big hug. "You really saved our lives back there!" she whispered into his neck,

"If it wasn't for you, Mum would be tearing us apart right at this very moment!"

As soon as Kim's mother and Casper had gone, Nick hurried over to them.

"What's happened?" he gasped, "Did you get into trouble?"

"Yeah, but it wasn't too bad!" Kim told him, "My mum was mad, but I think she's so pleased Jamie's been sorted out, she didn't go as ballistic as I thought she would!"

"I always wondered where he kept all those tricks he used," Nick said with a grin, "I just never managed to suss it out!"

"Well, Mrs Jennings has got them now, so Jamie won't be able to use any of them on poor old Casper," Kim said with satisfaction, as the crew began to take up their positions, ready to resume filming. Kim's mother was already standing near the river with Casper, and Jamie was there too, still looking furious and kicking at a tuft of grass. "And Mrs Jennings *and* my mum are going to be watching him from now on."

"Yeah, Mrs Jennings is pretty cool!" Nick agreed, "None of the other tutors we've had have been able to do anything with Jamie. They were all a bit scared of him!"

"Can we have silence on the set, please?" called the assistant director, "we're ready to begin the rehearsal."

Kim watched as her mother released Casper from his lead, and told him to sit down next to Jamie, ready to begin the scene. Casper obeyed her immediately, but Kim saw the retriever give Jamie a suspicious look.

"Action!" the assistant director called out.

"Walk on, Casper," Kim's mother said, and Casper obediently trotted along the river path next to Jamie. As Jamie launched into his speech about wishing he could keep the dog, Kim couldn't help noticing with dismay that Casper seemed a little edgy. He kept glancing up at Jamie nervously, as if he was expecting something to happen.

"Things are a bit difficult at home," Jamie went on, "my brother's got in with this gang, and they've got him into stealing and doing burglaries—" Just like before, he pulled his hand out of his pocket to pat Casper on the head. But this time, Casper immediately shied away, avoiding Jamie's hand, and began to bark loudly.

"Cut it!" Tony Allison roared, jumping to his feet. "What's that mutt playing at? Paul and the dog are *supposed* to be best mates!"

"Sorry." Kim's mother hurried over to Casper, who was still barking at Jamie, and grabbed his collar. "I think he must be getting tired or something."

"Tired!" Tony Allison repeated scathingly, "he's hardly done anything all morning!"

"What's the matter with Casper?" Sarah whispered anxiously to Kim, "Jamie couldn't have played another trick on him, could he?"

Kim shook her head, her heart sinking as she saw Jamie grinning smugly.

"No, I reckon Casper's just had enough of him!" she muttered. "Those tricks he played have made Casper nervous – that's why he wouldn't let Jamie stroke him. After everything's that's happened, he doesn't like him – and I don't blame him!"

"You know what they say, never work with animals or children!" Tony Allison was saying sarcastically, "Sorry, Jamie – *you're* OK – it's the mutt that's the problem!"

Jamie shrugged, obviously enjoying himself

again. "Maybe he's just not very well-trained," he suggested cockily.

Kim glanced at her mother, who didn't say anything, although she looked as if she'd like to. Kim knew that she wouldn't want to go running to the director, telling tales about one of the most popular actors on *North Park Avenue*. On the other hand, it wasn't Casper's fault that he was so nervous, it was all down to Jamie Marshall.

"I think that Casper's a little unsettled," Kim's mother said as calmly as she could. "Perhaps we could try the scene without Jamie stroking Casper?"

Kim knew her mum would much rather take Casper home for a break, but with a tight budget and an even tighter time schedule she knew it wouldn't be popular with the crew.

They tried the scene again without Jamie stroking the dog. At last it was over and Kim could breathe a sigh of relief.

"Right," Tony Allison yelled crossly, "I want that dog on his best behaviour for the night shoot this evening, or he's out on his ear! If he can't do the business properly, I'll find myself another dog who can!"

8

"But, Mum, what are you going to *do*?" Kim asked for the hundredth time.

Her mother sighed, as she walked back towards the river for that evening's night shoot. It was already getting dark, and the moon was a flat yellow disc in the blue-black sky. "Kim, I've told you already. All I can do is try to get Jamie to make friends with Casper again, so that they can finish the filming – that's why we're going up there a little earlier. And you don't have to tell me

it's going to be hard, because I already know it
is."

"Jamie won't want to," Kim muttered, glancing
over her shoulder at the retriever padding along
quietly behind her. "I know he won't."

"He'll have to if the director makes him," her
mother pointed out. "But you're right. Jamie could
make things very tricky if he decides not to co-
operate."

"I hate Jamie Marshall!" Sarah said indignantly,
"And I'm never going to watch *North Park Avenue*
again!"

"Me neither!" Kim added. "If Casper gets the
sack, it'll be Jamie's fault!"

"I know he's a brat," her mother said
thoughtfully, "but I can't help feeling a bit sorry
for him."

Kim and Sarah stared at her. "Sorry for *Jamie*?"
Kim said incredulously. "Why?"

"Well, he's only a bit older than you, and he's
got a lot of pressure on him, starring in a really
popular TV programme. And *he's* very popular
himself." Her mother shrugged. "I can understand
why he might have gone off the rails a bit."

Kim thought about that. She couldn't imagine

what it would be like if she suddenly became a TV star, and everyone knew who she was, and thought she was wonderful. Maybe being in that situation *could* make someone a bit big-headed and difficult to deal with. "Well, I wouldn't have cared if he'd been rude to *us*," she said, "Just as long as he'd been nice to Casper."

"True," said her mother with a sigh, as she headed towards the filming area. It was easy to spot because there was a blaze of light around it in the middle of the pitch-black countryside. "Oh well, your dad thinks the same as me. If Casper won't work with Jamie, we'll just have to pull out, and Tony Allison will have to find another dog."

"That's not fair, Mum," Kim grumbled. It was a cold night, and she wound her long, stripy scarf tightly round her neck to keep out the chill. "Why should Casper get the blame when it's all down to Jamie?"

"That's showbiz, I'm afraid, Kim!" her mother said dryly, "the star's always right!"

"Well, I think it stinks!" Kim said fiercely, and Sarah nodded in agreement.

There were only a few die-hard fans waiting

behind the barriers as they went over to the set, and Kim was pleased to see that, for once, Charlotte wasn't there. Everything looked much the same as it did by day, except that a couple more lights had been positioned and switched on to illuminate the filming area.

"Right, now I'm going to find Tony Allison, and tell him I need at least half an hour with Jamie Marshall!" Kim's mother said grimly, as she handed Casper's lead to Kim. "Keep Casper here with you until I get back."

As Kim's mother went off, Nick hurried over to join them. He was already in the clothes he wore to play Matt, but he hadn't been made up yet. The scenes to be shot that night were about Matt sneaking off the boat in order to go and burgle a nearby house, but being followed and stopped by Paul and the dog.

"Hi, you're early! Filming isn't going to start for about forty minutes."

"I know," Kim replied, "But my mum wants to try and make sure Casper and Jamie get on this time!"

"Oh." The smile vanished from Nick's face. "Well, that might be a bit difficult . . ."

"Why?" Kim and Sarah said together.

"Because Jamie's disappeared!" Nick told them with a faint smile.

Kim and Sarah stared at him. "What do you mean, *disappeared*?" Kim gasped, imagining that Jamie had wandered off into the dark countryside and got lost, never to be seen again.

Nick shrugged. "He does it every so often to annoy people! I reckon he's winding Mrs Jennings up, because she told him off this morning – she's running round like a nutter trying to find him!"

"But where's he gone?" Sarah asked. She looked past the lights, to the path along the river. It was so dark beyond the filming area, that it was impossible to tell where the river ended and the ground began. "He couldn't have gone for a walk, could he?"

"Oh, even Jamie's not that thick!" Nick replied. "He'll be around the set somewhere, he always is. But he's pretty good at finding places to lie low, and he always appears just before the filming starts, so he doesn't get into trouble."

Kim frowned. "But my mum's looking for him. If she can't stop Casper feeling nervous around him, they won't be able to work together!"

Nick shrugged. "Well, maybe that's another reason why he's disappeared!"

"I bet!" Kim said angrily. She stared round the set, but the only sign of Jamie was his black sweatshirt, hanging on the door handle of the boys' trailer. That gave Kim an idea. She grabbed the sweatshirt, and gave it to Casper to sniff.

"Find, Casper!" she told the retriever in a determined voice. "Find Jamie!"

Casper sniffed the sweatshirt, and then the ground, looking for a fresh track that could take him to Jamie. He did that a couple of times, and then took Kim off towards the river, keeping his nose to the grass.

Nick and Sarah hurried after them. "I don't believe this!" Nick said with a grin, "You never give up, do you, Kim!"

Kim shook her head. "I'm not going to let Jamie go round telling everyone that Casper's useless!" she said firmly. "No way!"

Casper made his way right across the set, then stopped by the river. He sniffed around a few times, stopped by the boat and then barked.

"D'you think Jamie could be hiding on the boat?" Kim asked eagerly.

"He might be down in the cabin," Sarah suggested.

"Could be." Nick frowned. "We're not actually filming in the cabin, though, so it might be locked."

"Let's see." Kim and Casper climbed on to the deck of the boat, followed by Sarah and Nick. Carefully Kim tried the door handle. It moved slightly.

"There is someone down there!" she whispered to the others, "I can see torchlight!"

"What shall we do now, then?" Nick asked, "run down there and surprise him?"

"No, I've got a better idea!" Kim pulled the door open a bit wider, and beckoned to Casper. "Go on, boy!" she said, pointing at the steps which led down to the cabin, "go and see what you can find!"

Casper bounded eagerly down the steps, and Kim, Nick and Sarah waited. Then, a few seconds later, they heard an angry voice yelling, "Get out of my way, you stupid mutt!"

"Result!" Kim whispered to the others, and they all began to laugh.

A moment later Jamie, holding a comic and looking very red-faced, appeared in the cabin

doorway, with Casper right behind him.

"Will you get this dog off me!" Jamie snapped, as Casper gave him a nudge in the back. "Ow!"

"What're you doing down there?" Nick asked with a grin, "Mrs Jennings is looking for you."

"And so's my mum," Kim added.

"Tough!" Jamie said rudely. "They can carry on looking, for all I care!"

He jumped off the boat before any of them could stop him, and ran off along the river path, away from the set. A second later he was swallowed up in the darkness.

"What's he doing?" Nick muttered anxiously, "we're not supposed to leave the set – it's pitch-black out there!"

"At least he's got a torch with him," Sarah pointed out.

Nick still looked worried. "I suppose I'd better go after him and bring him back," he said. "I haven't got a torch though."

"I have." Kim dived into her pocket, and pulled out her torch. "Mum told me to bring it just in case. We'll come with you."

They set off along the path in the direction in which Jamie had gone. The thin white beam from the torch wasn't really a lot of help, so they all took care to keep well away from the edge of the river, letting Casper, who was trotting along as sure-footed as ever, walk on that side.

"Where does he think he's going?" Nick murmured, annoyed, after they'd been walking for a minute or two. "I mean, he's got to come back this way sooner or later—"

"What's that?" Kim stopped suddenly at the sound of leaves rustling somewhere in front of them. She played the torch beam away from the river and into the trees, but there was no sign of Jamie.

And then they heard it. A loud SPLASH, followed by a faint, gurgling cry of "*Help!*"

Her heart pounding with terror, Kim grabbed Nick's arm. "Did you hear that?" she stammered, "Jamie's fallen in the river!"

9

For a second or two, Kim, Nick and Sarah were all so horrified, none of them could move. Then, with shaking hands, Kim dropped Casper's lead, and shone the beam of light over the dark water.

"I can't see him!" she whispered, "Do you think he's gone under?"

Nick had already torn off his leather jacket, and was pulling impatiently at the laces on his trainers. "Keep looking!"

"We've got to get him out!" Sarah gasped, "The

weir's not far down the river!"

"The weir!" Kim turned pale. She'd forgotten about the weir, but she knew how dangerous it was. If Jamie got swept down as far as the concrete dam, he would surely be sucked down into the whirlpool created by the strong current . . .

"Nick!" Sarah grabbed his arm. "You're not – you're not going in after him, are you?"

"I haven't got any choice – I know Jamie's not a good swimmer!" Nick shook her hand off, and kicked his trainers away. "Look, it'll be OK – I've done life-saving classes!"

"But it's dark out there, you won't be able to see—" Kim gabbled, feeling as if she was in the middle of a really bad nightmare.

"You'll have to keep the torch beam trained on me." Nick pulled his T-shirt over his head, and dropped it on the grass. "Sarah, you run back and get some help!"

"OK," Sarah agreed bravely, even though she would have to find her way back along the dark path without a torch.

"You'd better take Casper with you," Kim said, still frantically scanning the waters for any sign of Jamie. "He'll get you back to the set safely—"

Then she stopped, just as Nick was poised on the riverbank, about to dive in. "Listen! What was that?"

"What?" Nick asked impatiently.

"Wait, Nick!" Kim told him with a frown, "Don't go in! I heard someone laughing . . ."

She played the beam around into the trees near the river, and then gasped. Jamie Marshall was standing half-hidden behind a tall beech tree, doubled over with helpless laughter.

"You – you—!" Kim was so furious, she couldn't say a word.

"Of all the stupid tricks!" Nick, who was already shivering, grabbed his leather jacket, and wrapped it round him. "You prize prat, Jamie! I was just about to dive in to save you!"

Jamie laughed even harder. He staggered out from behind the tree, and over to the riverbank, keeping well away from Kim and the others.

"If – you – could – have – seen – your – faces!" he gasped between giggles.

"But – but we heard a splash!" Sarah said, puzzled.

"He must've heaved a big stone into the water or something," Nick said grimly. "Well, that's it!"

He stared at Jamie angrily. "He's gone too far this time – I could have been in the river by now!"

Jamie was laughing so much, he could hardly walk. He tottered over to the path, almost splitting his sides. "Got you, didn't I, Nick!" he spluttered helplessly, "You really fell for that one!"

"Come on, let's go," Kim snorted in disgust. She couldn't believe that Jamie had played such a childish – and dangerous – prank. What if Nick had dived into the cold, dark water? He could have got into serious difficulties.

"What's the matter?" Jamie teased her, "Don't you think it's funny? I do!" He took a step forward and pulled a face at Kim, but suddenly he stumbled, and fell. He disappeared immediately from view, and a second later there was a loud SPLASH.

Kim, Sarah and Nick stared at each other in amazement.

"This time he's really gone and done it!" Kim gasped. "He really *has* fallen in!"

"Help!" Jamie's voice floated to them through the darkness. He sounded absolutely terrified. "Help me!"

Quickly Kim shone the torch over the river. The

beam wasn't very strong, but they could just make out Jamie's head bobbing up and down, quite far already from the bank.

"There he is!" Sarah yelled, "And he's being carried down towards the weir!"

"I don't believe this!" Nick began pulling off his leather jacket for the second time. "Sarah, go and get help!"

"And take Casper," Kim added, keeping the torch beam fixed on Jamie's blond head just above the water.

Another loud splash made them all jump.

"Casper!" Kim screamed, her heart turning over with fear.

Casper had plunged into the river, and was swimming grimly through the dark waters towards Jamie, his lead trailing behind him.

"Good dog!" Nick called encouragingly, "Keep going, Casper!"

Kim was too frozen with fear to say anything. She ran along the riverbank, watching the retriever paddling towards Jamie, her heart in her mouth. She knew that Casper was a big, strong dog, but the river current was treacherous the closer they were swept along to the weir. What if Casper didn't have the strength to get himself and Jamie out?

Guessing Kim's fears, Sarah slipped her arm round her friend's shoulders, and gave her a quick squeeze. "Casper can do it!" she said quietly, "I know he can!" Then she hurried off along the dark path to fetch help, as fast as she dared.

"Casper's nearly there!" Nick shouted with relief, as the dog swam right up to Jamie, but Kim's hands were shaking so much she couldn't hold the torch beam steady. Nick took the torch from her, and shone it directly on to Jamie. "There he is, Casper!" he yelled, "Go for it, boy!"

Kim and Nick watched anxiously, hardly daring to breathe, as an exhausted Jamie flung his arm gratefully round Casper's neck, and they both set off on the long journey back to the river-bank.

"He's done it!" Nick murmured thankfully, "Casper's done it!"

"They're not back yet," Kim muttered, her face white with tension.

Casper was still swimming hard, but not as strongly as he had done before. It was obvious that the strain of pulling Jamie along with him was exhausting him, especially as they were going against the current.

"Keep going, Casper, *please*!" Kim prayed silently. The thought of both Casper and Jamie being swept away down to the weir was too much to bear . . .

"What's happened?" Nick said suddenly, in a dismayed voice, straining his eyes across the water to see what was happening. "Why have they stopped?"

Kim put her hand over her mouth. "I think they're stuck!"

"It looks like Casper's lead's caught on something under the water!" Nick said grimly, "a branch or something."

Kim trembled all over with fear as she watched the big dog straining to pull himself free without success.

"I'll have to go in and help them—" Nick began, but then Kim grabbed his arm.

"No – look!"

Jamie, exhausted and scared as he was, had obviously realised what was wrong, and was struggling to release Casper's lead from his collar. A second later the lead floated free, and Casper and Jamie were on the move again.

"We're going to have to pull them out," Nick said as the dog and the boy neared the bank, "they're going to be too tired to climb out themselves." He cautiously slid down the bank and waded a little way into the river. Kim followed him. The water was freezing cold, and quickly soaked right through the bottoms of her jeans.

"Don't go in too far!" Nick called anxiously, "it gets deep really quickly."

Casper and Jamie were coming closer now, and Kim could see how exhausted they both were. Casper was keeping going by sheer willpower and was panting heavily, and Jamie was shivering all over.

As the dog and the boy came nearer, Kim and Nick both reached out and took hold of them. Nick grabbed Jamie's sleeve, and Kim grabbed Casper's collar. Between the two of them, they hauled them out of the water and safely up the riverbank on to the path. They could see torch lights in the distance and hear voices, which meant that Sarah was on her way back with some help.

"Are you all right, Jamie?" Nick asked,

wrapping his leather jacket round the trembling boy, and Jamie just about managed a faint nod.

"Casper, you're the greatest!" Kim said shakily, throwing her arms round Casper's neck and hugging him, wet fur and all. "You're the bravest dog in the whole world!"

10

"Do you want another dog biscuit, Casper?" Kim asked, stroking the retriever who was stretched out lazily in front of the fire.

"Or maybe he'd like a bone," Sarah added, fondling the dog's silky ears.

"You two are spoiling him!" Kim's father said with a grin.

"I know, but he deserves it!" Kim replied. "If it hadn't been for him—"

"Don't!" said her mother with a shiver. "I'm

just glad Casper was there to help."

Kim jumped up and went into the kitchen, returning with a handful of dog biscuits. Harry and Spike, who were dozing next to Casper, also sat up, looking interested.

"All right, you can all have some." Kim handed the biscuits round, "but Casper gets two because he's a hero!"

It was the day after Casper had rescued Jamie from the river. Filming had been suspended for the day to give Jamie time to recover and to be checked over by a doctor. Casper, too, had been taken to the local vet, who had given him a clean bill of health.

"I reckon it was pretty big of Casper to jump into the river and save Jamie Marshall after all he's done to him!" Luke remarked. "And it was pretty stupid of him to fall in anyway!"

"I guess Casper just can't bear to see anyone in trouble," Kim said softly, fondling the dog's ears, "even Jamie Marshall."

"Maybe Jamie'll calm down a bit now and stop fooling around so much," Kim's mother said soberly. "After all, if he hadn't been playing a trick on Kim and the others, this would never have happened."

"I can't wait to see the newspapers tomorrow," Sarah said eagerly, feeding the retriever another biscuit. "I hope there are loads of pictures of Casper!"

"We had about fifteen journalists and photographers on our doorstep this morning, so there's bound to be!" Kim's father pointed out with a smile, as he went off into the *Animal Stars* office, followed by his wife. A few minutes later Luke went up to his bedroom, and Kim and Sarah were left alone with the dogs.

"Back to school in a few days!" Kim groaned, her arm round Casper's neck. "Oh well, I guess we've had enough excitement for a while!"

"Yeah, but there's just one thing I still want to know!" Sarah said solemnly.

"What?"

"How are you going to get Sooty through his catflap?" Sarah began to laugh. "I've asked you about a million times, and you haven't told me yet!"

"Oh, that!" Kim grinned too. "Yeah, I suppose I haven't really spent much time on my problem page – I've had other stuff to think about! But I've got a few ideas. Lucy could try propping the catflap open to begin with, and letting Sooty get used to coming in and out while it's open. Or she could try using some of Sooty's favourite treats to get him to come through. Oh, and I'll ask her if the catflap's got a clear window or not. Cats like being able to see where they're going, and if the window's not see-through, Sooty might not like it—"

"OK, OK!" Sarah laughed, holding up her hands. "Sounds like Sooty's going to be zooming happily through his catflap any day now!" Then she frowned. "Kim, d'you think Jamie and Casper will get on all right now?" she asked hopefully. "D'you think they'll be able to finish the filming tomorrow?"

Kim shrugged. "Who knows? It all depends on Jamie. We'll just have to wait and see . . ."

"Hi, Casper!"

As Kim's mother drew the car to a halt in their usual spot, not far from the set, Kim wasn't surprised to see that there was the largest crowd so far gathered behind the barriers. Everyone had seen the stories and photos in the newspapers, and had come out to catch a glimpse of the heroic dog who had saved Jamie Marshall's life. But what she *was* surprised to see was that Jamie Marshall was hanging around on the edge of the set, as if he was waiting for someone. When he saw the Millers' car arrive, he immediately hurried towards them. Kim and Sarah could hardly believe their eyes.

"Hi, Casper!" Jamie said again, bending down to wave at Casper through the car window. Then he glanced sheepishly at Kim and Sarah. "Hello," he muttered, turning red.

As Kim's mother opened the back of the car, Casper jumped out, wagging his tail, and pushed his nose gently into Jamie's hand. Jamie grinned, and rumpled Casper's shaggy head, and cameras began to click madly in the crowd.

"The press must be here again!" Kim whispered to Sarah.

"Oh, good!" Sarah said, "Maybe they'll take our pictures as well this time!"

"Jamie!" called one of the photographers, "Can you keep stroking the dog, and look this way, please?"

"How're you feeling today, Jamie?" a journalist added, notebook and pen at the ready.

"Jamie, Tony said no photographs or interviews with the press until after the filming's over!" Mrs Jennings said sternly, bustling over to them. Nick was with her, and he grinned and winked at Kim and Sarah, as they climbed out of the car.

"Can I take Casper over to the set?" Jamie begged Kim's mother, who looked surprised but pleased.

"Yes, of course." She handed him the lead, and

Jamie looked as pleased as if he'd just won the lottery.

"Jamie, we've heard rumours that the dog isn't particularly well-trained," another of the journalists called out quickly before Jamie and Casper could walk off. "Can you tell us what you think about that?"

Kim glared at the man who had the nerve to ask such a rude question after Casper had been so heroic. She guessed it was the journalist from the local newspaper whom Charlotte's father knew, although Charlotte herself was nowhere to be seen in the crowd.

"Actually, Casper's the most well-behaved dog in the whole world," Jamie said firmly, "and he's the best actor I've ever worked with!" Then he walked off, with Casper trotting along obediently beside him.

"I couldn't have put it better myself!" Kim whispered to Nick and Sarah. "Looks like Jamie's had a real change of heart!"

"I think what happened really shook him up," Nick confided in them as they walked over to the set. "He's been pretty quiet ever since. And then his mum came over to visit him yesterday – and

Mrs Jennings told her exactly what's been going on!"

"What happened?" Kim asked curiously.

"His mum said if he didn't sort himself out, she was taking him out of the show," Nick told them. "Jamie was pretty shocked by that, so I reckon he'll calm down quite a bit now."

Kim's mother and Mrs Jennings had walked on ahead, chatting, but Jamie stopped and looked round, waiting for Kim, Sarah and Nick to catch him and Casper up.

"Er – I just wanted to say . . ." Jamie began, then stopped. Kim waited in silence. Jamie might be turning over a new leaf, but she didn't see why she should make things *too* easy for him. "I'm – er – sorry about what happened before . . . About the tricks and everything."

"That's OK," Kim said generously, "I'm just glad you and Casper are friends now."

"Yeah, if it hadn't been for Casper . . ." But Jamie couldn't finish the sentence. He shrugged and swallowed hard. "Anyway, I hope we can be friends now too."

"Sure!" Kim said with a grin.

"Let's shake on it!" Jamie took his hand out of

his pocket with a smile, and offered it to her.

Kim took it willingly, and then gave a loud yell. "What – what's that?" she squealed, horrified, as one of Jamie's fingers came off in her hand.

"Sorry, Kim!" Jamie said, bending down to retrieve the fake finger. "That's one of my new tricks!"

Sarah and Nick burst out laughing and, after a second or two, Kim joined in.

"Don't worry," Jamie assured her, "I'm not going to play any tricks on set any more. I think I'll stick to acting from now on! And maybe one day I'll be as good as Casper!"

Casper barked loudly, as if he was pleased with Jamie's decision, and Kim patted the dog's head.

"You're a star, Casper!" she told the retriever, "A real *Animal Star*!"

SPIKE'S SECRET
Animal Stars 3

Narinder Dhami

When Kim Miller's parents start an agency training animals for TV and film work, she's delighted. She loves animals and she loves showbiz, and now Animal Stars is so busy, there's plenty of opportunity to help out . . .

Spike, the Millers' new mongrel dog, has just completed his first job – a TV commercial – and has become a star overnight. The first ad in a series, the Millers have to keep the storyline secret. But with all eyes on Spike, it's proving hard to keep the newspapers at bay – and some journalists will stop at nothing for a story . . .

COCO ON THE CATWALK
Animal Stars 4

Narinder Dhami

When Kim Miller's parents start an agency training animals for TV and film work, she's delighted. She loves animals and she loves showbiz, and now Animal Stars is so busy, there's plenty of opportunity to help out . . .

Animal Stars has an exciting new project – a top designer wants them to train some cats for his next fashion show. There's only one catch – the designer wants his own cat, Coco, to take pride of place on the catwalk. But Coco is a spoilt Siamese and very disruptive. Her training sessions are a disaster. Can Kim find a way to win Coco over, before she ruins the show?

MIDNIGHT THE MOVIE STAR
Animal Stars 5

Narinder Dhami

When Kim Miller's parents start an agency training animals for TV and film work, she's delighted. She loves animals and she loves showbiz, and now Animal Stars is so busy, there's plenty of opportunity to help out . . .

Animal Stars have been contracted for their first big budget movie: a legend about a mysterious black stallion. Midnight is perfect for the part! Visiting her mum on location, Kim befriends Caitlin, the daughter of the film's star, and, with Midnight's help, helps her overcome her fear of horses. But now Caitlin wants to go a step further and ride Midnight. Kim's not sure she's ready, but how can she say no to a movie star's daughter?

ORDER FORM

ANIMAL STARS series
by Narinder Dhami

All Hodder Children's books are available at your local bookshop or newsagent, or can be ordered direct from the publisher. Just tick the titles you want and fill in the form below. Prices and availability subject to change without notice.

Hodder Children's Books, Cash Sales Department, Bookpoint, 39 Milton Park, Abingdon, OXON, OX14 4TD, UK. If you have a credit card you may order by telephone – (01235) 831700.

Please enclose a cheque or postal order made payable to Bookpoint Ltd to the value of the cover price and allow the following for postage and packing:

UK & BFPO – £1.00 for the first book, 50p for the second book, and 30p for each additional book ordered up to a maximum charge of £3.00.

OVERSEAS & EIRE – £2.00 for the first book, £1.00 for the second book, and 50p for each additional book.

Name ....

Address ....

....

If you would prefer to pay by credit card, please complete:
Please debit my Visa/Access/Diner's Card/American Express
(delete as applicable) card no:

Signature ....

Expiry Date ....